GOODNIGHT GOON

A PETRIFYING PARODY

Michael Rex

G. P. Putnam's Sons

In the cold gray tomb
There was a gravestone
And a black lagoon
And a picture of—

R.I.P.

Martians taking over the moon

And there were three little mummies rubbing their tummies

And two hairy claws
And a set of jaws

And a loud screechy bat
And a black hat

And a skull and a shoe and a pot full of goo

And a hairy old werewolf who was hollering "Boo"

Goodnight tomb

R.I.P.

Goodnight goon

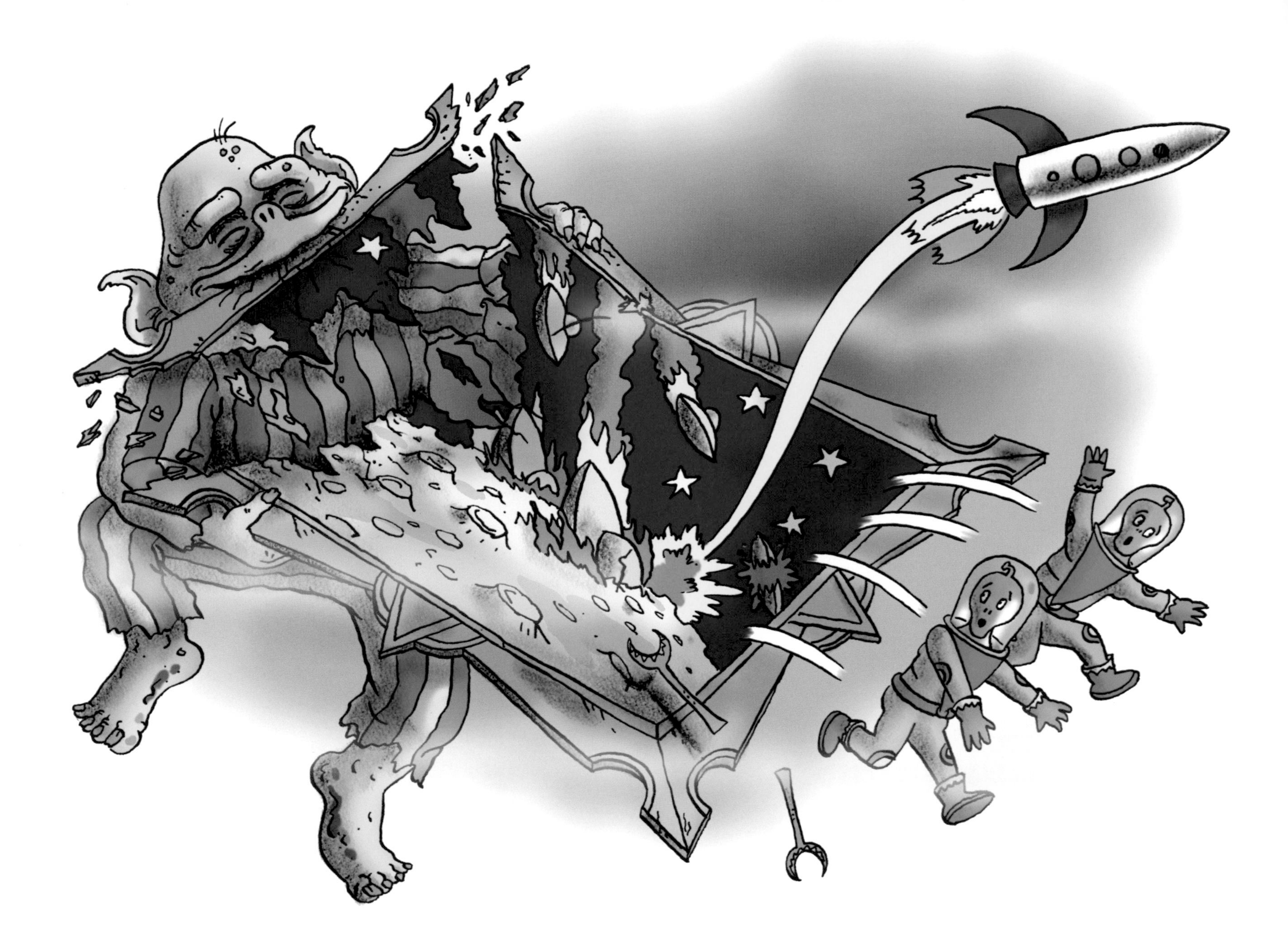

Goodnight Martians taking over the moon

Goodnight bones
And the black lagoon

Goodnight mummies
Goodnight tummies

Goodnight claws

And goodnight jaws

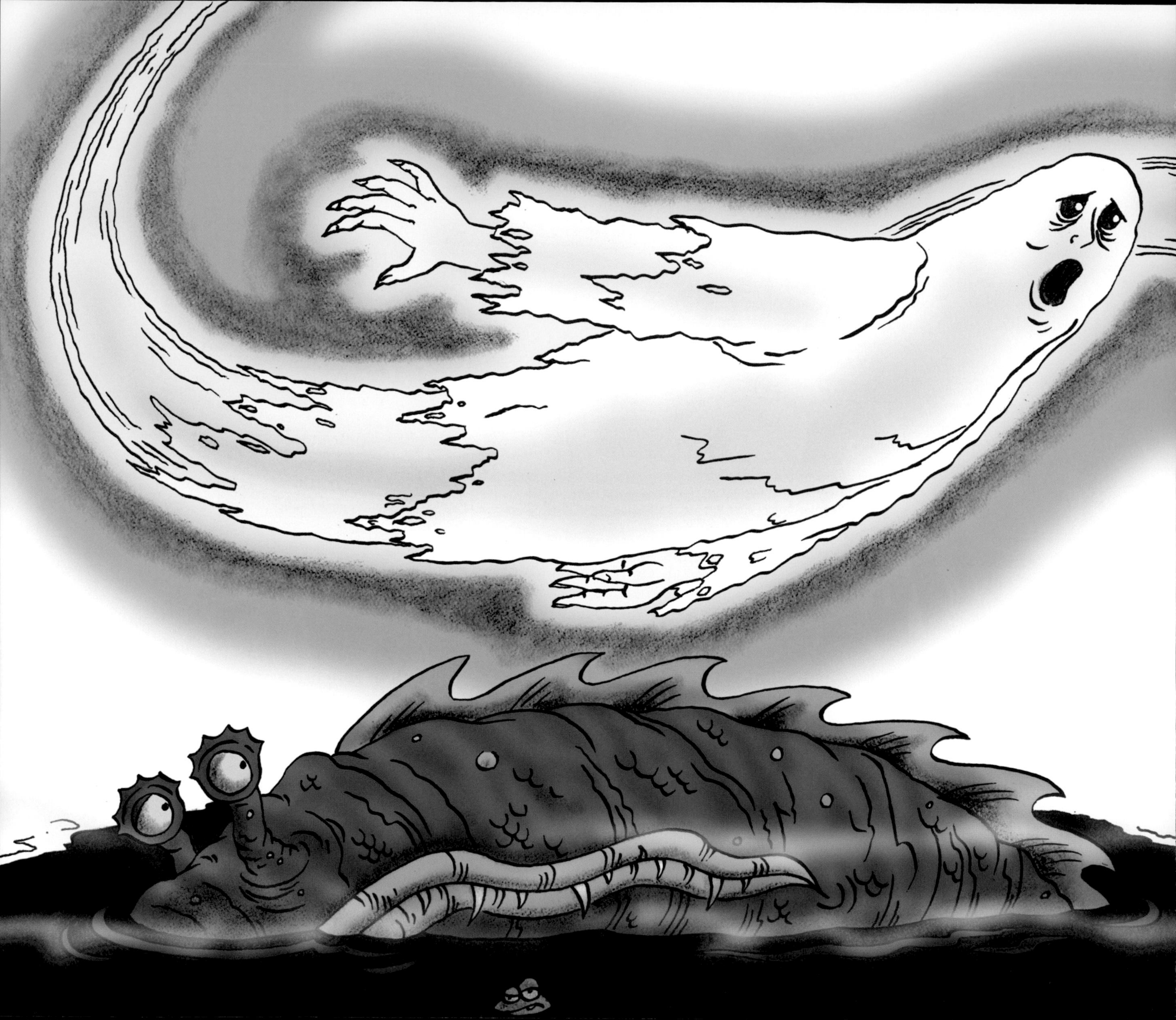

Goodnight moans
And goodnight groans

Goodnight screechy bat

And goodnight hat

Goodnight skull

And goodnight shoe

Goodnight creature

Goodnight goo

And goodnight to the old werewolf
hollering "Boo"

Goodnight you

Get under there

R.I.P.

Goodnight monsters everywhere

Just for Gavin

G. P. PUTNAM'S SONS
A division of Penguin Young Readers Group.
Published by The Penguin Group.
Penguin Group (USA) Inc., 375 Hudson Street, New York, NY 10014, U.S.A.
Penguin Group (Canada), 90 Eglinton Avenue East, Suite 700, Toronto, Ontario M4P 2Y3 Canada
(a division of Pearson Penguin Canada Inc.).
Penguin Books Ltd, 80 Strand, London WC2R 0RL, England.
Penguin Ireland, 25 St. Stephen's Green, Dublin 2, Ireland
(a division of Penguin Books Ltd.).
Penguin Group (Australia), 250 Camberwell Road, Camberwell, Victoria 3124, Australia
(a division of Pearson Australia Group Pty Ltd).
Penguin Books India Pvt Ltd, 11 Community Centre, Panchsheel Park, New Delhi - 110 017, India.
Penguin Group (NZ), 67 Apollo Drive, Rosedale, North Shore 0632, New Zealand
(a division of Pearson New Zealand Ltd).
Penguin Books (South Africa) (Pty) Ltd, 24 Sturdee Avenue, Rosebank, Johannesburg 2196, South Africa.
Penguin Books Ltd, Registered Offices: 80 Strand, London WC2R 0RL, England.

Published simultaneously in Canada. Manufactured in China by RR Donnelley Asia Printing Solutions Ltd.
Design by Marikka Tamura. Text set in OPTI Malou.
The artist used pencil drawings colored in Photoshop to create the illustrations for this book.
Library of Congress Cataloging-in-Publication Data
Rex, Michael. Goodnight goon: A petrifying parody / Michael Rex. p. cm.
Summary: A young monster says goodnight to all of the other monsters in his bedroom.
[1. Monsters—Fiction. 2. Bedtime—Fiction. 3. Stories in rhyme.] I. Title. PZ8.3.R318Goo 2008 [E]—dc22 2007016585
ISBN 978-0-399-24534-3
22 21 20 19 18 17